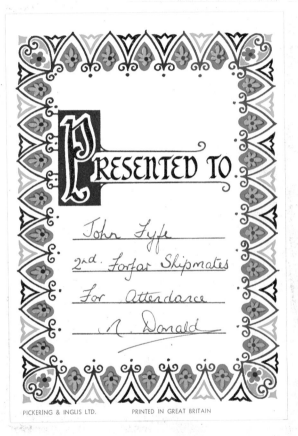

PRESENTED TO

John Fyfe

2nd. Forfar Shipmates

For Attendance

A. Donald

PICKERING & INGLIS LTD.   PRINTED IN GREAT BRITAIN

A DONKEY CALLED DANDO

A DONKEY CALLED DANDO

by
KIM SIMMONS

VICTORY PRESS
LONDON and EASTBOURNE

Printed in Great Britain for
VICTORY PRESS (Evangelical Publishers Ltd.)
Lottbridge Drove, Eastbourne, Sussex
by Compton Printing Ltd.,
London and Aylesbury

CONTENTS

CHAPTER ONE

THE DIPPER

Dicky's birthday present started the adventure. "Your wretched bird book!" complained Nina. "You can't think of playing any games now you've got that."

Dicky continued to turn the pages, murmuring the names of birds he knew. "Come and look here!" he demanded, ignoring his sister's grumbles. "Look at this smashing picture of an eider-duck— Jimmy Fergusson says he saw a whole lot of them down at the bay."

Nina came to look. Eider-ducks sounded exciting. The name made her think of the pink eiderdown which was on her bed. Eider-ducks ought to be pink birds, she decided, but when she looked at the bold black and white of the ones in Dicky's picture they were much more ordinary.

"They're just ducks," she said flatly; "my eiderdown is pink."

"It's made of nylon, anyway," Dicky told her loftily; "these are special sort of birds that live up here in the north, and I guess it's ages since anyone made an eiderdown of their feathers. I'm going down to Fence Bay to look for some, before Grandma thinks of something else for us to do. You needn't come if you don't want to."

Nina hated being left alone, so she dropped her ball, and grudgingly joined the expedition.

Grandpa's house was up a little lane which turned off the busy coast road. It was very quiet there among the trees, though the sound of the distant traffic was like a steady hum all day.

The other sound, which Nina loved, was the rush of water over big brown rocks. It swirled and eddied beside the lane on its way to the sea, and the children called it a stream, but Grandpa said it was a burn.

They loved being with their grandparents in Scotland while Mother and Father were away.

With his precious book under his arm Dicky ran ahead of his sister, but they had to wait a good many minutes before they could cross the main road in safety. Once across, the wide sweep of the fields, and the swampy land which edged the bay, looked lonely and inviting. "Just waiting to be explored," said Dicky.

Soon the sounds of the big road had dropped away into nothing, and the wind and the birds were their only companions. As they ran, some plovers rose quite close to them.

Dicky stopped in his tracks. "Wait a minute; there's a picture of those——"

He thumbed through his book anxiously. Jimmy would know what they were, he thought with a sigh. Jimmy was ten, a whole year older than himself, and Nina was only eight. But, as it happened, it was Nina who saw the eider-duck. Getting impatient with the bird book, she ran on ahead, jumping on the tussocky grass. A moment later she was on the beach, scuffing the fine sand, and picking up shells which lay in their hundreds along the tide line.

And then she saw them—a little family of ducks and ducklings swimming only a few yards from the shore. Most of them were a speckled brown but two were boldly black and white.

"They're here, Dicky! I can see them!" she shrieked. "They've got little eiderdowns as well—hurry up or they'll go out to sea!"

Dicky came running, and together they watched the small flotilla going steadily down the coast.

"I wonder if Grandpa knows they're here. He asked us to tell him when the terns came back, because then he'd know it was really summer."

"He doesn't come down here," said Dicky; "it's too far for his rheumatics. We'll take him home some shells."

They idled about in the sun, listening to the larks above their heads and watching a whole regiment of oyster-catchers out on the mudflats.

"They all turn the same way just like soldiers, and they've got the biggest orange beaks I've ever seen."

Suddenly Nina had caught some of Dicky's enthusiasm for the birds, and that brought Jimmy Fergusson into her mind.

She didn't like Jimmy much. He lived in one of

the fishermen's cottages down by the shore, and he was always telling them that they were townies.

Dicky didn't seem to mind it, and begged to be allowed to go off with Jimmy digging bait, but Nina ran back to the house when the two boys got together.

Now she had an idea whereby her beloved Dicky could prove himself as good as any country boy.

"Is there any bird in your book that Jimmy says he hasn't seen?" she asked.

"A dipper," answered Dicky promptly. "He says they're awful hard to see; they can keep right down under the water if they want to, and stay there ages."

"Dippers are stream birds—burn birds," he told her. "They live around where there are waterfalls and things. Jimmy showed me the picture when he went through my book. He said, 'That's one I never set eyes on, but there must be some up the glen.'"

Up the glen! Nina's eyes sparkled. She had wanted an excuse to follow the steep track above Grandpa's house, ever since they arrived, but Dicky had wanted to be on the shore every day.

"Let's go and look!" she urged. "Let's go up higher and higher until we find one, and then Jimmy can't call us townies any more."

Dicky closed the book and sat back on his heels. He looked across the flat land to the clustered houses of the village and the great, dark hill which rose behind them and seemed to tower into the sky.

"It's a long way up there," he said dubiously.

"Doesn't matter," declared Nina, who was suddenly determined to see a dipper at all costs. "We can't get lost if we follow the water all the way up and down. We'll go home now because it's dinnertime, and we'll explore while Grandpa's reading the paper this afternoon."

Suddenly feeling enormously hungry, they ran all the way home.

The spicy smell of gingerbread greeted them, and the patty pans and cake racks told them that Grandma was having one of her baking sessions.

"Good bairns!" she said approvingly. "In nice time for lunch. Go and wash, and call your grandfather; he's making his back ache, with that wretched mower."

Dicky ran out towards the sound of the machine, pulling seaweed and shells from his pocket. Grandma would call them rubbish, but Grandpa wouldn't. He would turn them over and trace the lovely curving patterns with his fingers, and say that sea songs lived in the pink hearts of them.

Grandpa stopped the mower and listened with approval to the story of the eider-duck family. It was all Dicky could do not to mention the dipper, but he decided that it should be a big surprise.

Nina had thought the same thing, and, as she ran through the hall when the meal was over, she heard a scrap of conversation which told her that they had chosen just the right afternoon for their dipper hunt.

Grandma was speaking on the phone, assuring someone at the other end that she would be baking two more batches of cakes for the church tea. "The children?" Nina heard her say. "Oh, they're no trouble; they entertain themselves wonderfully all day, and never get under my feet!"

"Well, there!" said Nina to herself. "We'll be doing a good turn, not getting under her feet."

They knew the beginning of the road up to the glen quite well, but as they went higher it seemed a very still and mysterious place, even on a summer day. But the stream was alive. It poured down a narrow cutting between high banks green with ferns, and it rushed round great rocks which tried to bar its way.

They had to scramble along as close to it as possible, in case any dippers could be seen on the rocks, but the only birds were chaffinches, high above their heads.

Suddenly Dicky shouted, "There's a bridge! We could get over the other side!"

Nina stood still and looked where he was pointing. The wooden bridge, very high above them, was old and weathered, and in a moment they were scrambling up towards it.

Dicky raced across first, calling back, "There's a stile and a path! It might go somewhere good. Come on! Let's see!"

It was a field path, leading away from the glen and round the shoulder of the hill. Now they could see the whole of Fence Bay below them, and the islands ringed with blue water.

"That's where we were this morning!" Nina cried. "There's the boat that goes to Arran, halfway across, and it looks so tiny!"

They were so busy looking at the vast view that they were considerably startled by a voice behind them. Neither of them had realized that a thick hedge and a small clump of trees concealed a small, low house.

The voice came from a very old, wrinkled person who was peering over the hedge at them.

"What might you two be doing up here?" she asked. "It's not often bairns get up so high."

"We're exploring," answered Dicky briefly.

"Ye're up to see the poor donkeys, I'll be bound."

"What donkeys?" asked Dicky and Nina both together. "And why are they 'poor'?" added Nina, interested.

"Because they're 'no-good' donkeys, mostly, and he buys 'em cheap and sells 'em dear," grumbled the old woman. And then she turned away and disappeared into the cottage, without another word.

"Donkeys!" breathed Nina. "I love donkeys—I wonder where they are."

"Farther along the path, I guess," said Dicky; "but if it's a horrible man that buys them and sells them, we don't want to get told we're trespassing."

"Well, we could just *see* them," pleaded Nina. "Perhaps they're in a field, and people come to

B

buy them."

She started to run on, and Dicky followed.

"There's nothing here at all—only sheep," he said after a while.

"Let's go just as far as that gate," Nina begged, and then suddenly she shouted, "There there! I can see some!"

Dicky saw them, too. They were walking up beside the wire which divided off part of the hill—five grey donkeys with their ears moving as though they had heard the children's voices.

Dicky reached the gate first, and the donkeys came up at a trot. They certainly did seem rather old and shaggy.

"They're super!" said Dicky, wishing he had something to feed them with.

"We can only scratch their foreheads for them," he said sadly, "but we'll ask Grandma for some crusts, and come again."

At last they tore themselves away and raced back along the path, fearing Grandma's displeasure if they were late for tea.

The glen seemed very cool as they scrambled over the bridge, and if Nina's sandal hadn't come undone just then perhaps they would never have seen the dipper. Halfway across the bridge, she stooped down, blocking Dicky's way, and, looking down at the rocks below, he saw a flash of wings.

A small bird went flitting down just above the water. It was such a dark brown that it looked almost black, but its white breast showed clearly, even at a distance.

"Look, Ninny! There he is—the one we came up here to see—it simply *must* be a dipper."

Dicky sat down on the old bridge and Nina crouched beside him, afraid to speak any more lest they frightened it away. It was certainly dark and white, but how could they tell it was the right bird? Then suddenly it lived up to its name and began bobbing up and down on the rock at tremendous speed, making short runs towards the swirling water.

"It's dipping! It's dipping! It's the right one!" shouted Dicky, forgetting his caution, and the tiny bird flew and shot down the stream like an arrow.

CHAPTER TWO

DONKEYS AGAIN

Even Grandma seemed interested in the dipper, though she frowned a little when they said that they had been up the glen.

"Can't come to any harm; they're sensible children. Can't get lost," said Grandpa, answering her unspoken thought. "So you don't want Jimmy Fergusson to have it all his own way, eh?" he added, his eyes twinkling.

"He probably hasn't seen the donkeys, either," boasted Nina, and then Grandma really did exclaim.

"You've been all up there! To Ross's place! No wonder you're hungry, and you must be tired out!"

"We're not! We're *not*!" cried Dicky. "We want to go up again tomorrow and take them some crusts. Do say we can, Grandma! They're lonely, and they *need* us to talk to them!"

"Do they indeed!" A look passed between Grandma and Grandpa, but as usual he was on the children's side.

"Keep 'em busy," he said; "you'll know where they are. Time they get back from there they'll be too tired to get into mischief."

Of course, they wanted to see Jimmy Fergusson that evening before they went to bed, and this time Nina was anxious to go as well.

"But we won't tell him about the donkeys," she said as they ran down the lane. "He might want to climb over the gate and ride them, and get everybody all upset."

Dicky thought that was very likely. "We won't even say we crossed the bridge," he promised.

This time they went away from Fence Bay, up the road towards the houses and the post office.

There they had found narrow cuttings which went between garden walls and led right out on to the rocks. Jimmy's house was built just above the beach, and Dicky and Nina liked to chase down the passage, each trying to be first out on the sea wall.

Dicky was well ahead, and he rounded the corner at the seaward end at top speed.

Nina didn't see what happened; she only heard two shrieks and a thud.

When she raced out of the passage, Dicky was just picking himself up, and a large elderly lady was sprawled across the narrow pathway which edged the rocks. Around her lay tubes of paint and a twisted easel.

A camp stool was turned on its side, and canvas and brushes were down among the seaweed.

"Ah! you gummerel children!" cried the old lady as she struggled to rise. "Can you not come quietly, without knocking a body over?"

Nina ran to help, and Dicky, red in the face with

shame, came, too.

"I'm awfully sorry," he gulped. "I wasn't expecting——"

"Neither was I," retorted their new acquaintance grimly. "I expect folks to walk about like sensible creatures."

They set the stool up and helped her on to it, pulled the easel straight and began to collect the scattered tubes.

"Oil paint!" noticed Nina, and thought anxiously, "Dicky's gone and knocked over a real artist!" She stood up with her hands full of paints, and met the steady grey eyes of the painter.

"Turn your head a little to one side and let me have a look at you!" Nina did as she was told and saw Dicky scrambling up from the rocks, clutching a canvas which was liberally streaked with brown and green.

"Remarkable! Remarkable!" the old lady was saying, and she wasn't looking at Dicky or her picture. She was just staring at Nina's long, straight hair which Mummy called 'ash blonde' and Dicky called 'mousey'.

"Can I move now?" asked Nina meekly.

"Sensible question. Sensible child. I must paint you some time. Where d'you live?"

Dicky set down the canvas carefully against the wall and replied for Nina, who was struck dumb at the idea of being painted.

He explained that they were staying with Grandpa and Grandma Murray.

"Mr and Mrs Murray, is it? Well, you can tell them you've bowled over Ada Murchison, but no bones broken and no harm done!"

And then her glance fell on Dicky's grubby knee on which a bright red patch was widening.

"Good gracious, boy! There *is* harm done! That's a nasty cut you have; come along and get it seen to."

Miss Murchison got stiffly up from her stool, and, leaving it where it stood, she led them a short way along the path and then opened one of the big old doors which were set at intervals in the sea wall. 'Water gates', Jimmy Fergusson called them, and now they were all going through one as though it was the most ordinary door in the world.

"Shut it behind you, or the wee dog will get out."

The 'wee dog' was a very old cairn terrier which came eagerly to greet its mistress, and to sniff the children suspiciously.

"Angus won't bite," said Miss Murchison, and she led them into the high, narrow house which had tall windows looking out to sea.

"It's *super* in here!" whispered Dicky as she bade them wait in a rather old-fashioned kitchen while she went to get Dettol and a bandage. Nina looked round, sniffing the mixed smell of cooking and turpentine, and wondering at the number of potted plants crowded on the windowsills.

There were pictures, too. Every bit of wall space had its sketch or oil painting of the sea, the rocks, and sea birds.

They were gazing at them when Miss Murchison came down.

"So you like my art gallery?" she said, looking pleased.

"I like birds," said Dicky. "And I like your painting!" said Nina quickly.

"Diplomatic!" chuckled the old lady. "Here, boy —bring that knee of yours nearer the sink."

She was abrupt, but they didn't feel in the least afraid of her, and while she washed and bandaged the cut they told her all about the dipper.

"Jimmy Fergusson!" she exclaimed with a little snort of distaste. "He's always in mischief!"

"I think he could be nicer than he is," said Nina slowly. "He's awfully selfish, and he's not very happy sometimes—I think it's because he doesn't believe in Jesus."

"How d'you know?" demanded Miss Murchison crisply.

"Because he told us so one Sunday when we said we'd been to church with Grandpa." Dicky wriggled his sore knee because the bandage was tight.

"That's a pity, but people can change, you know," Miss Murchison reminded them. "Maybe you'll find a way to help him to change, one of these days."

Nina shook her head. "He just laughs at us," she declared.

Miss Murchison smiled down at her. "But you can pray for him when you say your prayers, and maybe God will find a way."

She picked up the Dettol bottle and turned towards the door.

"Want to come and see some more pictures?" she asked, and lumbered away without waiting for an answer. The children followed her to the steep, dimly lit staircase.

Up they went and came to a great light room with pictures all around its walls. There were landscapes and portraits, and delicate drawings of birds, but most of all there were photographs. Photographs of children and of babies. Black babies, white babies, laughing ones and crying ones, and Nina was enchanted.

"Why do you take so many?" she asked, as she toured the room in delight.

"Because I paint for pleasure, but it's the photographs that make the money, and one has to live in this expensive world."

Puzzled, Dicky asked why photographs made money and Miss Murchison explained carefully about children's portraits used in advertising.

"I have some little models that I take pictures of over and over again," she said; "they get quite used to the camera."

"Do you pay them?" Dicky wanted to know.

"I pay their parents, usually," she answered, "and then the advertisers who use the photographs pay me."

Dicky would have asked a lot more questions but the sound of a chiming clock made Miss

Murchison ask what time they went to bed.

"You'd better be off," she told them, "or Mrs Murray will be on my tracks."

They did not go to the water gate again, but were shown out of the front door which opened into the passage they had run down so many times.

"Goodbye," said the old lady kindly; "you may come and see me again some other time, but more gently please."

She closed the door, and they decided that Jimmy Fergusson must be forgotten for the moment.

"It was wizard in there," said Dicky, going as fast as his bandaged knee would allow. "As we didn't hurt her, I'm jolly glad I knocked her down."

Grandma was shocked when she heard of their latest adventure.

"You really must be more careful!" she exclaimed. "Miss Murchison, of all people! And she's so heavy to fall, too."

"Well, at least you got in to see her pictures, which is what many folks around here would like to do!"

Grandpa put down the seed catalogue he was studying and looked at them both as though he noticed for the first time how untidy they were.

"I don't suppose she wanted to photograph either of *you* in that state!" he said.

Nina, on her way upstairs, turned and looked down at him, tossing her long hair back and trying to look dignified.

"Miss Murchison said I was remarkable," she announced.

"Did she, indeed! Well, that might be taken several ways!" answered her grandfather, but Dicky was more pointed. "Hippopotamuses are remarkable, but they're not beautiful," he told her, and pushed her up to bed.

The next morning there were no arguments as to where they should go after breakfast.

The donkeys, they were sure, were looking for them, and they could hardly wait while Grandma rummaged in the bread bin and found them some crusts.

"You musn't worry them, mind," she said, "or Mr Ross might be cross."

She found two apples and a little packet of biscuits.

"Those are for you. Now, don't go giving everything to the donkeys. I get the good food for you and not to be given to four-footed beasts."

She stood at the door and waved to them as they turned up the lane. Nina waved back and blew a kiss before they reached the corner. They knew quite well that, although Grandma sounded stern, any 'four-footed beast' in trouble would claim her immediate attention.

The way up the glen seemed shorter this time, but although they kept stopping to watch for the dipper no little bobbing bird came in sight. Once across the bridge and out in the sun again they began to run. They looked curiously at the old woman's cottage but she was nowhere to be seen either.

"No dipper and no old woman," said Nina. "I hope we didn't dream the donkeys."

But the donkeys were certainly no dream. All five were clustered round the gate, looking as though they were really waiting.

"Oh, you darlings!" cried Nina, but Dicky had reached the gate before her. Five grey and brown noses came pushing round him, and Nina was crying, "Wait for me! Wait for me! Don't give them all the bread."

They broke it up as small as possible, to make it last a long time, and Nina tried to give most of hers to a shy old donkey who certainly looked rather thin.

"He's not very pretty but he looks anxious——" she was saying, when suddenly she broke off and gave a cry of delight.

Up the hilly field came another donkey, a tiny one, very dark and dainty. He walked with little careful steps and nodded his long ears as he came towards them.

"A baby donkey!" cried Nina, nearly falling over the gate with excitement. "He must be a baby; he's so much smaller!"

"I don't think he's a baby exactly; I think he's a child donkey!"

Dicky climbed up to sit on the top bar and get a better view.

"Why did he come when we've used up all the

bread?" Nina wailed, and then with joy remembered the apples.

"I'll eat mine and leave lots of core," she said. "Cores are all right for four-footed beasts."

Dicky did the same, and together they tried to coax the neat little donkey to come close. At last he took a step forward, and then another, and she threw the core towards him. He sniffed it suspiciously, and then to her delight he picked it up.

Seeing that there was no more for them, the donkeys drifted away, and the children sat down on the short turf in the sun and ate their biscuits.

"He's so tidy, that little donkey, and he's so brown," murmured Dicky, lying down flat to stare at the sky. "He's a dandy compared to the others."

"That's his name," said Nina suddenly. "Dandy. No, Dando—that's a gorgeous name for a donkey. Tomorrow I'm not going to throw him a core; he'll have to come and take it from my hand."

Like Dicky she lay flat and looked up at the great, blue dome of the sky, seeing the little brown donkey in her mind. "If I had a donkey," she said dreamily, "I'd always be reminded of Jesus riding one into Jerusalem."

Dicky sat up to have another look at them, but the sunny field was empty. "They've gone away now," he said.

"I wish Dando could be ours to care for," sighed Nina.

CHAPTER THREE

THE HOUSE IN THE TREES

"I wonder where the Ross's farmhouse is. We haven't seen anything up here except the old woman's cottage, and the hill looks quite empty." Dicky ate his last biscuit, squashed the packet flat and stuffed it into a tiny hole in the turf.

Nina watched him thoughtfully as he prodded it down. "If we followed round the wire fence we'd probably find it," she said; "the donkeys went off somewhere round the bend of the hill."

"Let's go and see. We've got ages of time before dinner, and the wire will show us the way home like the stream does."

They ran downhill for a little way, and then the fence turned upwards again, right round the shoulder of the hill, till the field of sheep was out of sight.

"There's a shed." Dicky pointed to a low building half hidden in a little hollow. "That's where the donkeys live when it's wet, I guess," he said. "And there's a haystack just beyond it, outside the wire."

A few yards farther and the posts they were following took a sudden dip into a little valley. "Just a crease in the hillside," Dicky called it, and there they could see trees, farm buildings, and a white-walled house.

"We've found it," said Nina, stopping; "I don't want to go any farther. If that man buys the donkeys cheap and sells them dear like the old woman said, he's probably nasty. He might be fierce. He might have big dogs. He might——"

"All right, you're scared." Dicky thought the half-hidden farmhouse looked rather still and lonely, but he didn't admit it. Instead, he had a bright idea which would save them the trouble of going all the way back.

"There's a little track leading down," he pointed out; "it goes down and down as far as I can see, so it must finish somewhere. I can see the sea and a little bit of beach which must be Fence Bay—if we just follow the track we simply have to get there."

Nina hesitated. There were thick trees below them, and beyond that the sea lay calm and blue, but the little piece of beach Dicky had seen looked a long way away.

"I don't think Grandma——" she began, but Dicky wasn't waiting for her, he was already running and calling her to follow.

His idea seemed a very good one till they had gone through two steep fields with an easy gate between. Then trouble loomed ahead for Nina because the next field was full of bullocks.

"I'm not going on!" she cried. "I'm not—I'm not!" Her voice rose in panic, and Dicky didn't feel too certain about the bullocks himself. But, looking back the way they had come, the hill seemed to loom larger than ever. It would be a very long way home.

They stood there in the summer stillness, feeling very much alone. The gentle cooing of collared doves came up to them from the trees, and the bullocks stamped just beyond the hedge.

"I'd rather go on than go back," said Dicky. "Look, there's a big thick hedge over there; it might be the side of a lane."

They padded across the short turf and peered through the leafy barrier. Joyfully they saw that Dicky was right. A slide down a steep bank deposited them in a cart track, which surely led down towards the sea.

Once more the trees closed round them as they ran, and then quite suddenly they came to old walls and dilapidated sheds.

"Old stables, I guess," said Dicky, stopping to swing on a half door and to peer into the dusky shadows, where pieces of forgotten harness hung.

But Nina was impatient. "I can hear the road now," she declared; "it can't be far—that sounded like a bus."

Now, great rhododendron bushes bordered the track, bright with their mauve and pink blossoms, and between them were glimpses of mown grass.

"There's a house!" Dicky whispered it because he had a feeling they were trespassing, and they both crept to a hole in the bushes and peered through.

A great white house was there in the sunshine, and a car stood in the drive.

"Let's run," whispered Dicky. "This bit of a

lane turns into that big drive, so there must be a way out."

At last they neared big white gates beyond which cars flashed by, but they did not feel happy till they were through them and stood panting on the grass outside, looking across to the sea.

"Blue Bay Convalescent Home. So that's what that house is!" Dicky read the big name-board by the gate and wondered why they had never noticed it before.

"What you doing?" said a voice suddenly, and Dicky swung round nearly knocking Nina down. Beside the gatepost with his hands in his pockets stood Jimmy Fergusson.

For once, Dicky wasn't pleased to see him.

"Exploring," he answered briefly.

"Trespassing!" said Jimmy with a grin.

"We aren't, then!" cried Nina, suddenly angry. "Trespassing is when you go where you know you're not wanted, but we got there by accident. Anyway," she added with triumph, "we saw a dipper yesterday, and you said you hadn't ever seen one yet!"

"You never! You're story-telling," jeered Jimmy, with a maddening expression on his freckled face. "There's no burn for dippers down this part of the hill—you just saw a wee wren dooking about among the leaves."

Now it was Dicky's turn to be angry. The naturalist in him was insulted.

"It was a dipper. A dipper! A *dipper*!" he yelled,

C

squaring his fists at Jimmy. "It was up the glen, and you dare say it wasn't! We're not townies any more—and I guess you haven't even seen the donkeys."

The minute that he had shouted the word 'donkeys' in his excitement, Dicky regretted it. Nina clapped her hand over her mouth as if to smother the word, but there was no getting it back.

Jimmy was astonished. "The donkeys!" he cried. "So you've been all up there? I got in and rode one once, and old Farmer Ross caught me and walloped me."

"We don't get in." Nina sounded very superior. "We're only going up every day to feed them and talk to them."

Jimmy made a face. "Not much fun, that," he said crushingly, as he turned to watch the traffic before running across the road to the lonely beach. Dicky was still very cross, but Nina suddenly remembered what Miss Murchison had said about helping Jimmy, and she felt at that moment that he would be very hard to help.

They stayed on the grass by the gate, glad to see him go, but once on the other side Jimmy stopped and shouted across.

"You won't be able to feed them much longer, anyway," he called. "I've heard old Mr Ross is selling them this week, and he's selling the lot this time."

"Who to?" called Nina in a stricken voice, and she was not comforted by Jimmy's answer.

"Guess he'll sell them for beach donkeys down in England, and they'll get walloped if they don't go fast enough!"

The rumble of a passing bus drowned anything else he might have said, and as it came by so close to them Nina looked up and saw Grandpa in it.

He waved, and pointed towards home. Dicky, catching sight of him at the last moment, thought he looked upset about something.

As they went home, Nina was only seeing Dando, little, neat, dark Dando, being whalloped because he didn't go fast enough.

She thought of the old donkeys, too, with their shabby coats and soft grey noses, but it was Dando who made her feel fierce and angry. Perhaps Jimmy had only said it to tease them, she told herself, but suddenly she remembered the old woman in her lonely croft above the glen. It was she who had muttered, 'buys them cheap and sells them dear'.

Nina ran on, just longing to tell Grandpa about it and to urge him to save Dando. Even Grandma would be sympathetic, she was certain.

They had a long way to run. Blue Bay Convalescent Home was a lot farther from home than they had imagined, and presently Nina slowed to a trot and then a walk. "I've got a stitch in my side," she said miserably as Dicky waited for her.

By the time they came to the familiar houses they were both feeling rather footsore.

"Have ye been away on your travels again this morning?" asked a kindly voice, and there was Mrs

Wallace who kept the little shop on the corner. She was outside, arranging boxes of oranges and bananas and eggs on her trestle table, and the sight of her made Nina feel better.

Mrs Wallace was as thin as a beanpole and her wispy hair was always untidy, but she had a face that was all kindness.

"She has pretty eyes," Dicky had said when they first met her; "they crinkle at the corners."

Mrs Wallace put down the oranges she was arranging and beckoned them in for a chat, but Dicky hesitated.

"Grandpa was on the bus, and I think he wanted us," he explained; "we might be by later on for some of Grandma's messages."

"Always welcome, dearie," said Mrs Wallace, and then she caught sight of Nina's woebegone face.

"Something the matter, is there?" she asked, but did not wait for an answer. "Nothing's half as bad as it seems at first," she said, giving Nina a reassuring pat, and Nina was quite sure that she for one would understand about Dando.

'Nothing's half as bad as it seems at first.' The words came back like an echo to Nina when they found Grandpa waiting for them at the door.

"Come in quickly," he said. "We couldn't think where you had got to, and Grandma and I have to catch the next train to Glasgow."

He was not cross, only serious, and Dicky asked at once, "Is something wrong?"

"It seems very wrong at the moment, but we

hope that it will be better presently." Grandpa took
them into the dining-room without even telling
them to go and wash, and they saw that the meal
was only laid for two. Mr and Mrs Murray had had
theirs already.

"Now eat up quickly while I tell you what has
happened."

Grandpa put ham and salad on Nina's plate and
absent-mindedly pushed a dish of jelly towards
Dicky.

"It's Uncle Max," he told them; "he and Aunt
Mary have had a bad car accident and they are both
in hospital. Thank God, Jane and Susan and little
Maxie weren't hurt, but Grandma and I will have
to go up and be with them each day till we see how
things are going. Auntie Jean will be with them at
night, but she works in the library, you see, so she
can't be there in the day time. Of course, we shall
want to be visiting the hospital as well."

"Will Uncle Max be all right?" asked Nina, suddenly finding her salad very hard to swallow.

"I believe he will," Grandpa told them, "and
Aunt Mary, too, but I'm afraid it may take them a
long time. We must ask God to help them get better, and to bless the doctors and nurses who care for
them."

Just then Grandma came in wearing her navy
blue hat, which always meant she was going to
church or to Glasgow.

"Now, you children will be all right," she said
briskly. "Mrs McPhee is in the kitchen, and she

will stay till we get home this evening, and come every day till this emergency is over. You be good children and do what she tells you."

"Who's Mrs McPhee?" asked Dicky anxiously.

"She's a kind soul who has helped us for years, on and off," Grandpa explained. "She cooks and cleans if ever Grandma isn't well, and you mind you obey her. She'll be off for just an hour each afternoon, but you two are old enough to amuse yourselves for that short time, and if you're in any trouble go to Mrs Wallace."

Ten minutes later, Grandma and Grandpa were hurrying off to the station and Mrs McPhee had joined the children at the front door to wave them away.

She looked a nice person, Nina thought, and her bright red and blue apron was certainly cheerful.

"Well, we'll all have to look after each other for a little while, won't we?" she said, as she closed the front door, and added, "Before you know where you are, your Auntie and Uncle will be away to a convalescent place."

It was only when she said 'convalescent place' that Nina remembered Dando, and at the same time she had an idea which gave her a queer, jumpy feeling inside. Even if the donkeys were sold and went south to England, Dando should not go with them.

CHAPTER FOUR

THE HIDEAWAY

The taxi had disappeared, and Mrs McPhee was washing the dishes before Nina could think out her idea properly. She went and found Dicky, who was in the sun-room. "I want you to help me!" she said urgently. "I'm going to save Dando so that he won't be sold, but I can't do it all by myself."

"We couldn't steal him!" exclaimed Dicky.

"We're not going to steal him; we're just going to hide him till the others are all gone, and then we'll take him back and put him in the field again. I guess they'd keep him because he's so little, if all the rest were sold."

"But we couldn't hide him," objected Dicky; "there's only the shed, and it's too full with the tools and the mower."

"We won't hide him in *our* shed," cried Nina, jigging up and down with excitement. "We'll hide him in those lonely old stables behind the convalescent home! We wouldn't be trespassing, because they're right outside the garden, and anyone could use that lane."

Dicky was impressed. "But there'd be feeding him," he said.

Nina's face fell; that problem had not occurred

to her. She realised that Grandma's crusts were only treats for a hungry donkey.

"Hay," she suggested after a minute. "I think Jimmy buys it for his rabbit hutches."

"Grass!" cried Dicky. "We could pull armfuls of it!" Dicky was getting enthusiastic. "We'd better go this afternoon," he said. "We can ask Mrs McPhee for some crusts and tell her Grandma lets us feed the donkeys. We'll have to hurry, because we might not catch him first try."

Mrs McPhee had started work on a pile of ironing when they appeared at the kitchen door. "Donkeys?" she said. "Oh yes, your grandpa told me you liked to feed them. He said you were up there this morning but you stayed far too long. Your grandma was in a fuss and no mistake when you didn't come in to your dinner. Your grandpa had to eat his in a hurry and get on the bus. He had to put off some folks who were coming to supper tonight—when folks is wanted they're never on the phone."

She switched off the iron and went to investigate in the bread bin.

"Sure you won't be too tired?" she asked, hesitating at the larder door. "It's a long walk to do twice in one day."

"We're not tired," Nina told her hastily. "Grandma says we've got cast iron legs, and it's shady up the glen."

"I'll have your teas ready at half past five, then," said Mrs McPhee, coming out of the larder with a bag. "No sense in dragging you in early if you're happy out of doors."

Dicky took the bag, wishing he dared ask for biscuits as well, but Nina had a brilliant idea. "Could we have a carrot?" she begged. "There's one little shy one that would love a carrot!"

"Never satisfied, are you?" Mrs McPhee seemed as if she was about to say 'No', but then she changed her mind. "Can't see any harm if your grandma's got a few carrots. Here's one that's not too special." She took it from the vegetable basket, giving it a rub on her apron.

They thanked her hastily and made for the door, but as they got outside a thought struck Dicky.

"What are we going to lead him with? None of them have halters on."

They went out into the lane to discuss it, because that was where Mrs McPhee expected them to go.

"Grandpa hasn't got any rope that I know of, but there's Grandma's washing line," suggested Nina.

Dicky shook his head. "It's plastic," he said; "I guess it wouldn't tie properly. He might get tangled up in it."

They sat down on the green bank, feeling that Dando was doomed. "I'll hate feeding them now we know they're all going," Nina said. Then suddenly she shouted, "Belts! That's it—belts!"

"A belt isn't long enough," Dicky told her gloomily.

"One belt isn't, but three or four would be! There's your mac belt and mine, and the one off my green dress!"

"All tied together they might do, if we had some string to make them hold," agreed Dicky. "Come and let's fetch them. I'm sure Mrs McPhee would let us have some string; Grandpa does."

But Mrs McPhee was not in the house when they ran back. She had gone to pick some parsley from the bed beside the lower hedge, and had found that Mr Gipps next door was gardening on the other side. She stopped to tell him about the accident, and Mr and Mrs Murray's trip to Glasgow, so no one answered Nina's 'Coo-ee!' as the pair raced upstairs.

The mackintosh belts were easily slipped off, but the one on Nina's dress had been stitched and needed snipping. Dicky stumped about restlessly while she did it.

"Who's there?" cried a startled voice from below. Mrs McPhee was standing in the hall with her hand over her heart, and she looked very relieved when Dicky put his head over the bannisters. "I thought you were a burglar upstairs!" Mrs McPhee sounded cross.

"We're really going now," said Dicky hastily.

"Make the most of your donkeys," said Mrs McPhee, softening a little. "That Mr Ross mostly gets rid of them in the spring."

"So it's true!" cried Nina when they got out in the lane again. "Jimmy wasn't teasing us, and the old woman was right, too! We've just got to catch Dando and hide him before tonight!"

They ran through the glen faster than ever before, and only stopped a fleeting moment on the bridge to look for dippers.

"None there," said Dicky; "we mightn't ever see it again." He scrambled across into the meadow and they ran helter-skelter.

At first they thought the donkey field was empty, but, when they climbed up to balance on the gate, Nina saw some grey ears waggling beyond hurdles that were evidently built as a windbreak.

The children called and whistled softly and the grey ears swung forward. One by one, the donkeys appeared.

Nina counted them. "Only four," she said; "I'm certain there were five this morning, and I can't see Dando anywhere."

They ran along by the wire a little way, calling, and four disappointed donkeys trailed after them. And then they saw him. He was down in the hollow where the fence curved round towards the house, and he was rolling happily on the warm turf.

"Dando! Get up quickly—we want you!" Nina's voice was shrill with anxiety. Dando's head perked up and with a final kicking of legs he came upright, shaking himself before he stepped carefully towards them.

Then began a tantalising time while Dicky lured them all towards the gate with small pieces of crust. At last they were clustered round Nina, while Dicky joined the belts together as best he could.

Of course, he had no string! Mrs McPhee's

sudden appearance had made them forget it entirely. Luckily, the green cotton one from Nina's dress tied in easy knots, and Dicky pulled hard to make the knots tight. "Ready!" he said. "You stand by to undo the gate when I've got him."

Dicky went forward with the carrot in one outstretched hand, and with the other hand he pushed away the crowding grey muzzles that tried to take the tit-bit from him.

Dando scratched his cheek with a dainty hind hoof and stayed where he was. Cautiously Dicky moved on, the belts hanging over his shoulder, offering the carrot with soothing words.

The small donkey backed away a little and then stood uncertain. A grey one, catching Dicky unawares, butted him sideways and made him drop the carrot.

"Oh, you silly! You silly!" cried Nina in a frenzy of anxiety. But Dando, seeing the carrot rolling, came forward suddenly. As he bent his head to get it, Dicky flung himself upon him, grabbing the startled little animal round the neck and yelling to Nina to come and help.

Luckily, Dando calmed down as he found arms round his neck and Dicky holding him firmly. Nina tied their 'halter' securely and gave the furry ear closest to her a kiss.

"We've got you, darling Dando, and now you'll be safe!" she told him, and tried to lead him to the gate.

But Dando thought otherwise. He planted his

four little hoofs firmly and stood stock-still. The children coaxed and pleaded and pulled. They were hot and sticky and afraid now, because the terrible Mr Ross might appear from the direction of the farm at any moment.

Then Dicky had an idea. "There's the rest of the bread the other side of the gate," he said. "Go and get it and feed the grey ones, and see if we can make Dando jealous when he sees them all eating."

It worked. Suddenly Dando went forward, and, dropping the bag to keep the others busy, Nina struggled with the wire loop which fastened the gate. Pushing and pulling, they dragged him through.

"We've done it, and no one's heard us——" Nina began thankfully, when suddenly one of the grey donkeys began to bray.

"Heehaw-heehaw." It was like a trumpet blowing to call the farmer, and in sudden panic the children urged Dando downhill.

Being out of his well-known pasture seemed to make him adventurous, and in a moment he was trotting with Dicky holding his halter and Nina running alongside. Every few yards she looked over her shoulder, fearing to see a large, angry man striding down towards them. But the Scottish hillside lay peaceful in the sun, and no one came.

It seemed a much shorter way down the hill this time, because they were going so fast and were certain of the way.

About fifteen minutes later Dando's small hoofs

were clicking lightly over the grey tiles of the old stable floor. He swung his ears and looked about a little nervously as they went into the shadows of the old building.

"You tie him to the manger, and I'll go across and pull him some grass." Dicky slipped out into the sunshine while Nina tied the loose end of their halter round the manger bar. Then she put her arm round Dando's neck, leaning her cheek against his warm, furry face.

"We'll come for you first thing after breakfast," she promised him, "and if there's no one about we'll take you for a walk up the lane."

Then a horrid thought struck her. The little donkey would be thirsty. Perhaps he was thirsty already, and she had no idea where they could find water for him. She let go of Dando with the idea of searching for a bucket, or perhaps a stable tap, but a sudden sound made her stand still with a fast-beating heart. Footsteps were coming along the lane—not the light scuff of Dicky's sandals, but heavy boots with a firm tread.

As they came nearer, she heard a man begin to cough.

CHAPTER FIVE

THE TRUTH ABOUT DANDO

Panic seized Nina. For no reason at all she was certain that the man with the cough was the cruel farmer, Mr Ross. Somehow she must get out of the stable without being seen, and warn Dicky not to come through the gap with handfuls of grass.

The steady steps came nearer. Perhaps the farmer might go right by, but Nina did not dare to risk his coming into the stable and finding her there. It would be so difficult to explain that they were not really stealing the donkey.

Beyond a farther stall there was a window from which the glass had long since fallen. The frame swung on sagging hinges and it was not very far from the floor.

In a flash Nina was scrabbling her way up, finding a tiny foothold in loose bricks and dragging herself astride the sill. The next moment she dropped with a soft thud on to soft earth.

Keeping close to the wall, she edged towards the lane. The footsteps had stopped. Was Mr Ross looking into the stable, and if so would he see Dando in the shadows?

She looked anxiously across towards the gap where Dicky was sure to appear in a moment, trying to think how she could warn him and stop him calling to her.

And then she saw that he was warned already; he, too, must have heard the cough. His brown face and tousled hair showed slightly between some hawthorn bushes, and his bright eyes were looking towards the stable door.

A wave of relief stilled Nina's fear for a moment, but only a moment, because a gruff voice said, "What is it, Rusty?" and at that moment a large brown dog appeared round the corner of the wall.

If she had stopped to think, Nina would have seen it was a gentle red setter, but at that moment she was certain it was a hound sent to hunt her down.

She turned and ran. Plunging across the thick grass, slipping into a tangled ditch and scrambling out again, she made for the rhododendron bushes.

For a few yards the dog went after her, till a slight whistle from the lane made him stop and then disappear again, but Nina did not know. She thought he was still coming, and she scrambled under bushes with the stiff branches dragging her hair and catching her jersey.

On the other side of the green barrier she found herself in a gravelled yard at the back of the big house.

Through open windows came sounds of voices and laughter, though there was no one to be seen. If only she could get round to the drive and the big gates without being noticed, and then out onto the well-known road!

She dashed across the yard and into the shelter of a shed which stood close to the house wall.

Surely the great dog wouldn't see her there, she thought, but in a moment she had another alarm. The back door of the big house opened and a trim young girl in a blue overall crossed the yard to some washing lines. She left the door wide open, and passed so close to the shed that Nina was certain she would hear her heart thumping.

But the girl went straight on, and Nina heard her say, "Well, what do you want? You don't belong here, you know!"

Nina couldn't know that a grey tabby cat had risen sleepily from beside a clothes post, asking to be stroked; all she thought of was the brown dog, and that Mr Ross was probably not far behind it. She dashed for the open door, through a large kitchen, and on down a passage, meeting no one.

Her light sandals made scarcely a sound, but someone in high heels was coming down a staircase which seemed all too near.

Nina stopped. Seeing that a big cupboard door close to her was slightly open, she slipped inside.

It was a vast cupboard and seemed to be full of small coats hung high on hooks, and there was a smell of mackintoshes close to her face.

She drew the door to after her, leaving it ajar as it had been, and stood with her breath coming fast, as she peeped out into the passage.

D

She wished desperately that Dicky was with her, but in the dim closeness of the cupboard her fear of the dog receded.

The high heels clicked away into the distance. Voices, and the sound of children laughing and one crying came from rooms beyond.

In the kitchen she had just left, somone was singing. Perhaps it was the girl who had hung out the washing.

It was. A moment later she came along the passage, said something under her breath about 'never will shut doors', and closed the cupboard with a bang, turning the key.

Any courage that Nina had left was blotted out. In the stifling darkness when all light and air were cut off, she turned into a wild thing.

Screaming, she kicked and beat the door till the panels shook. It seemed hours, though it was only minutes, before her muffled cries were noticed in the big, busy house.

She heard people running and calling, and a voice of authority said, "Well, which one can it be? They were all on the lawn or in the playroom just now." The key turned and Nina tumbled out into the light.

A gasp of astonishment came from three young women in blue overalls.

Someone very tall and dressed in grey caught Nina by the shoulder, saying quite calmly, "Well, this is a surprise! Would you mind telling us how you come to be in our coat cupboard?"

Suddenly Nina found she was trembling. All the excitement of the day and the last few frightening minutes seemed to make her legs turn to jelly. She pushed her hair out of her eyes with a dirty hand and looked up at her questioner, not knowing how to answer.

The brown eyes that met hers were very kind, and suddenly she took courage.

"I suggest you come to my office and tell me all about it," said the grey lady, "and it seems to me that you could do with a nice cool drink of lemonade and a biscuit. How about it?"

"Yes, please!" cried Nina, suddenly finding her tongue, and she followed her down the passage from which big, light rooms opened on either side. She caught a glimpse of a rocking-horse in one, and a teddy bear and a train lay just inside the door of another.

"But I thought—I thought this was Blue Bay Convalescent Home," she said, puzzled, as they turned into a sunny room with a large desk and a wide view out over lawns.

"Why, yes, it is—a convalescent home for little people under seven. That's why it gets rather noisy at times." A series of yells and shrieks of laughter came from upstairs, as though to prove it.

Nina sank into a large armchair and gratefully took the tall, cool glass that was given her. A blue-clad nurse carrying a bouncing toddler passed the open window, and half a dozen small children in bright red, green and yellow pinafores ran by.

"Those are a few of our 'nearly well' ones," said the grey lady. "My name is Miss Henderson, but you had better call me Matron, and I think it's time I knew what kind of scrape brought you to visit us."

So Nina told her story, and she told all of it, beginning where it really began with Jimmy Fergusson and the dipper.

Matron listened, not interrupting, but every now and then she frowned and tapped on the desk with her pencil.

"So you see," finished Nina rather anxiously, "we just had to save Dando from being sold this week! We couldn't bear to think of him being walloped because he didn't go fast enough, and we'll take him back when the others are all gone—truly we will! If you just let him stay in your old stable a day or two—that is," she added sadly, "if the man with the dog hasn't taken him already."

Miss Henderson looked at her with a sudden, lovely smile. "The man with the dog must have been Mr Oddie who does our garden," she said, "and he loves children. If he called the dog Rusty, well that's *our* Rusty, just out for a walk. Here he comes, by the sound of it!"

A little scratch and whine outside the door made Nina sit up straight, and when the matron opened it Rusty bounded in.

A moment later he had his feet firmly planted in Nina's lap and was trying to lick her face.

"And to think I was scared of you!" she cried, winding her arms round his neck.

"Which goes to show," Miss Henderson told her, "how wrong one can be about a lot of things. I do understand what you felt about Dando, but several matters must be explained." She made Rusty sit down beside her and then she leaned forward, fondling his long ears and talking to Nina as though she was another grown-up.

"We all make mistakes," she said, "and a terrible lot of them are made because people half hear things, and then add a bit from their own imagination, and pass it on. Mr Ross *does* have donkeys all the winter and get rid of them in the spring, and he *does* buy them very cheaply if they aren't given to him. They're all old, tired, sad donkeys, who need a bit of petting and good food and care through the hard winter. Then he finds them good homes where they can just keep someone's paddock grass down for the rest of their days. He has to get rid of each batch, you see, because there are always others coming to the end of their working days and waiting to come to him for a bit of cossetting."

"But Jimmy Fergusson said they were to go on the beach!" cried Nina, "and the old woman said 'buy's 'em cheap and sells 'em dear!'"

"Jimmy Fergusson's a classic example of getting hold of the wrong end of the stick. A lot of them *were* beach donkeys and Mr Ross buys them cheaply to prevent them being put down when they can't do a day's work any more. Old Moreg up at the croft is a poor thing. She sees the dark side of everything, and she is too muddled to understand why they come and go. She can only think that a farmer is out to make money, though actually she has lived rent free on his ground for twenty years."

There was silence in the room except for a fly buzzing up the pane.

Nina began to feel ashamed and silly, although part of her was very relieved as well.

"But Dando!" she cried. "He isn't old and worn out. What will happen to him?"

"Dando's mother had an accident before he was born," Miss Henderson told her. "She hurt her leg, and was sent to Mr Ross for him to take care of it. She is better now and has gone home. Dando will be sold when he is a little older. I expect that in a few weeks Mr Ross will be looking out for a good home for him, but he will certainly be sold at the right price for a healthy young donkey. I haven't seen him since he was two weeks old; we'll go round to the stable now and see how he's getting on."

She stood up and Nina looked at the clock. "Oh dear—it's nearly five already!" she cried. "Mrs McPhee will have our tea ready, and she'll be cross if we've not arrived by half past. It's going to take ages to get Dando up to the field again so that Mr Ross isn't cross, too!"

"I think we can manage it so that nobody is cross." Miss Henderson took Nina down the passage. "There!" she said, pushing open a door. "Go in and have a good wash, and let's see if we can get all this hair tidy."

"Oh! it's all for the babies," cried Nina, delighted with the row of small, low wash-basins. Each had a bird or an animal in bright colours above it, and the same picture was by every hook on which towels hung.

"Everyone knows their own towel even if they're too small for names or numbers," explained the matron, finding a clean towel from a drawer.

Five minutes later, neat and clean again, Nina felt much better. To her surprise, Miss Henderson proceeded to call the nurses and children together.

"Come and see a little visitor we have in the stables!" she said. "I know all the children will love to meet him."

She took Nina's hand and led the way out of the front door and round by the side of the house. The girls in blue followed, looking mystified, and with them came a toddling, running, laughing tribe of small children.

"It's like the Pied Piper of Hamelin!" thought Nina, her eyes bright with excitement.

Some of the small girls and boys looked pale and frail, she noticed, but they were all happy, and they fought to catch Matron's free hand or to get Rusty by the collar.

As the whole band turned into the lane and came in sight of the stables, Nina shouted, "Dicky's there! I must go and tell him," and with a swift glance to ask Miss Henderson's approval she raced on ahead.

Dicky had been lurking in the doorway and as

he heard her flying footsteps he came out, looking anything but pleased.

"What did you go tearing off like that for?" he began. "The man only stopped to light his pipe."

Then he saw the advancing troop, and his eyes widened with alarm.

"It's all right!" panted Nina. "It's all *right*! Dando's safe, and he won't ever be walloped. I'll tell you all about it presently."

When Miss Henderson joined them she said kindly, "So you're Dicky who has helped in this bit of well-meaning kidnapping! I'll drive you both home in a few minutes. Mr Oddie and Jock the garden boy can persuade Dando into our old van and drive him home, too, and explain why he vanished, and then I think everybody will be happy."

Dicky wanted to ask a dozen questions as they went into the stable. The way things were turning out was beyond him altogether.

"Oh! Isn't he a darling!" chorused twenty voices, and Dando looked up from the little pile of grass at his feet, his ears twitching with surprise. The children surged forward. A small, bold boy went to pat him and the rest followed, smoothing him with tiny hands.

Dando didn't seem to mind at all. "I knew they'd love him!" said Miss Henderson, and taking the tiniest from the arms of a nurse she set her gently on the donkey's back.

"Ride!" cried the baby. "Gee-gee!" and Dando

never moved except to reach down for another piece of grass.

It was difficult to get them away from him, but Mr Oddie was sent for. He heard the story briefly, and with some amazement, and then Dicky and Nina had to leave.

"I'll get you home with five minutes to spare," Miss Henderson promised as they got into her car. "And I think there's no need to trouble Mr and Mrs Murray by telling them of your adventures tonight," she added. "They are good friends of mine and I know they have trouble enough just now."

"Is Mr Ross a friend of yours, too?" asked Dicky, wondering.

"A good friend and our nearest neighbour," Miss Henderson began, when Nina suddenly leaned over from the back seat and said eagerly, "Wouldn't he give you a donkey for the children to ride, then?"

Miss Henderson drove swiftly up the busy road, and it was a moment before she replied. "I'm certain the children would love one," she said at last, "but the give-away ones are too old to want to have riders any more, and some are touchy-tempered now."

"But Dando!" cried Nina. "Dando would be good with them!"

"Dando," said the matron, "is a young donkey who will fetch a good price, and I'm afraid the management committee of the children's nursing home wouldn't vote money to be spent on buying him."

And that seemed to be final. She stopped the car at their turning and opened the doors. "Run," she said, "and make your peace with Mrs McPhee."

CHAPTER SIX

WHITE ELEPHANTS

"Well, some people do leave it to the last minute when they know other people have been getting their teas ready," was all Mrs McPhee said, although she looked very hard at the clock.

The children clattered upstairs to wash, anxious not to be asked any questions, and Nina found her legs were aching quite a lot after such an up and downhill day. Perhaps they were not so cast iron as Grandma had supposed, but she didn't mind them aching, because she had a joyful feeling inside about all the donkeys, and Dando in particular.

In her heart she said a little prayer of thanks to God because they would all be found happy homes. "Please help us to help Jimmy to be happy, too, by believing in You," she added, certain that her prayer would be heard.

It was Dicky who had the idea which set them thinking hard again. "Guess that management committee wouldn't say 'No' is someone *gave* them a decent donkey," he said, when Mrs McPhee had set down their plates of beans on toast and bustled out to the kitchen again. "Guess that matron wouldn't say 'No', either."

"But nobody could give them one unless they were rich."

"Listen!" said Dicky. "I've got an idea—just you listen."

So Nina listened, and was astonished at his wisdom.

"People raise funds," Dicky told her. "We could do the same. Dando will be up in the field for a little while yet; that matron said so. We could have a jumble sale for him, like Mummy's Guild did for the old people's outing, and then go to Mr Ross with the money before anyone else does."

Nina rocked on the edge of her chair and looked at him with admiration. "It's a wizard idea!" she said. "We'll tell Grandpa about it in the morning; he might give us that woolly waistcoat he says is too small."

But they had no chance to talk about Dando or the jumble sale next day. In the morning Mr and Mrs Murray had a rush to get through breakfast and catch the early train.

Uncle Max, they said, was doing well, but Aunt Mary was poorly. As for the babies, they had been as good as gold, but were naturally upset. "They'll probably come here while your aunt and uncle are convalescing," Grandpa told the children.

"Convalescing" reminded Dicky and Nina of yesterday's adventure, but they both knew it wasn't the time to start on that story. In any case, Mrs McPhee came in, puffing from riding her bicycle, and wanting to know about the invalids. So once more the children waved their grandparents away, and turned indoors to decide what they would do.

The steady hum of the vacuum cleaner told them that Mrs McPhee was doing the bedrooms, and they knew that she was too busy to be thrilled about the jumble sale. "I vote we go and see Mrs Wallace," said Dicky. Mrs Wallace was just the right person, they decided; she belonged to Grandma's Women's Guild, so she must know all about jumble sales. They dashed up to the room above, where Mrs McPhee was marching up and down the faded carpet.

"Have you any messages for Mrs Wallace?" shouted Dicky.

The sweeper sighed to a stop. "Well, that's thoughtful. Your grandma did say she'd left a list."

She gave them Grandma's shopping bag and the list. "And I want you to get some stamps for me, from the post office," she said. "There's also a note for the butcher. You needn't hurry back."

"Good," said Dicky, when they got outside. "That's three people we've got an excuse to ask. Mrs Thingummy at the post office always talks to us. If she's busy we'll just look at postcards till she isn't."

"Mrs Butcher's nice," remembered Nina. "I've seen her. She's got babies, and she has the pram round the side. Babies grow out of clothes—she might have some of their old ones."

They went to Mrs Wallace first.

"So your grandma's away to Glasgow," she

greeted them with her usual warmth, and offered them each an ice lolly.

"May we eat them here and talk?" asked Dicky, as she checked through the list and began to put the things into Grandma's bag.

"Sure you may. What are you doing with yourselves today?"

"We're having a jumble sale," announced Nina. "That is, we're getting things for it, and we want to have it soon because it's for a *very* good cause, and we thought you'd know all about raising money."

"Well, that's a lot all in one breath!" Mrs Wallace sat down on an apple barrel and began deftly sorting through a box of tomatoes.

"I can't remember that we ever played at jumble sales when we were small," she told them. "But real live jumble sales take a lot of work. If you just want to make a little to give to a charity I don't see any reason why not, and just one stall would do you. There's the little shed round the side where Mr Wallace used to keep his motorbike—now would that do to have it in? There's some tea chests and an old box or two would serve to put things on."

"Oh, Mrs Wallace, you're an angel!" Nina enfolded her in a somewhat sticky hug, the lolly getting dangerously near her hair.

"That's a smashing idea! It's right on the main road! Could we put a notice in your entry?" Dicky went out to survey the possibilities, and Mrs Wallace prepared to get on with her work.

"What did you say it was for?" she asked Nina. "If it's genuine I'll give you a few potatoes, and there's a little blue jug indoors that's got a chip in it."

Nina swallowed hard. 'What's it for?' was a question a lot of people were likely to ask, and she wondered whether they would be able to answer it clearly. And would everyone really agree that the convalescent home needed a donkey?

"Well, it's for some poor little children, really—ones that haven't been well and have had a bad time——" she began, when a customer took Mrs Wallace's attention.

"I see—convalescent," she said over her shoulder, and she turned to select a cabbage.

Nina ran out to join Dicky, and together they looked at the little shed. It had long since lost its doors, and it was plainly visible from the road. More than that, the bus stop was only a few yards away. Three customers were keeping Mrs Wallace busy, so they waved to her and set off towards the post office. They did not wait there, because it was already full.

But 'Mrs Butcher' was both chatty and amused. Her husband heard of their sale 'for a good cause' with a friendly chuckle and sent them through to the back of the shop while he cut off some chops.

His wife was busy washing, and rows of small white garments and nappies already hung out in the garden beyond.

The babies were out there, too, kicking happily

in their double pram.

"Come to see the twins, then?" said their mother, as though that was what people usually came for, but, when Nina started to explain, she was interested. "A little stall for a children's charity? Oh, yes, of course I'll find you something. Come round this afternoon and I'll have it ready."

They left the shop, feeling very elated. On the way home they collected an armful of children's old books and paperbacks, and a lampshade with a kink in it. Dicky had seen someone hurrying out to her dustbin with them and had intervened.

"Don't throw those away!" he cried urgently. "We're looking for things to put on a stall."

"Well, what an idea! I suppose you may as well have them to play with. This spring cleaning does turn out a lot of rubbish!"

She piled the books into his arms, and Nina had to take the shopping bag and the lampshade as well. But Dicky had not only collected jumble; he had collected an idea as well. "Spring cleaning!" he cried. "I guess everyone's doing it now. We'll go to doors and say, 'Are you turning out for the spring cleaning? We'd like things for our stall'!"

They took their trophies to the garden shed before they went indoors with the shopping. "I do wish Jimmy was nicer," said Dicky with a sigh as he closed the door; "we could have asked him to help us and had a lot of fun. Do you think God will really help him to change, if we keep on asking?"

"I guess He will," said Nina with certainty;

"there's a story about friends asking in the Bible—
those ones who tore a hole in a roof so that they
could bring someone near to Jesus to be made well.
Perhaps the invalid didn't really believe in Jesus
till it happened."

Some of Mrs Murray's friends had been a little
surprised at the children's activities that morning,
but most of them had found some small things,
glad that the children had something to keep them
busy and happy while there was such sad trouble
in the family at Glasgow.

"I doubt Mrs Murray knows they're going door
to door," said one lady to her husband, as she
watched them down the lane, but she had given
them some old lace doyleys, and a vase with 'A
Present from Rothesay' on it, all the same.

"Do you want any crusts for the donkeys today?" asked Mrs McPhee as she gave them their
meal, "or have you got tired of them already?"

"Not tired of them; but we're doing something
else," answered Nina happily.

"Well," she said, putting down their hot plates,
and going to get her own, "don't stay indoors now
that the sun is so lovely. I'll be away for an hour as
soon as I've washed up, so don't get yourselves into
trouble in that time."

"We're having a sale——" began Dicky, when
the doorbell rang. Mrs McPhee hurried away, and
by the time she came back they were talking about
dippers.

As soon as the meal was over, they ran down to

E

the butchers.

"Ah! You two! Come for the white elephants?" he said. Nina looked blank, and Dicky decided that he was teasing.

"If you've got a white one, we'd like it," he said, "if it isn't too big."

The butcher chuckled his deep chuckle, and called his wife.

"They're not elephants, but they're white," she said cheerfully, handing Nina a paper bag filled with outgrown baby clothes; and the pair left, thoroughly puzzled. They decided to do the houses on the shore road next, and immediately Nina thought of Miss Murchison.

"She's so nice, she's sure to give us something. Perhaps she's got one of her little pictures she's made a bit of a mess of."

"Or some of those pot plants that are all over everywhere," said Dicky hopefully.

They turned down the sea lane, and found it pleasant to stand on Miss Murchison's doorstep, listening to the terns crying, while they waited for an answer to their knock. Then they heard footsteps and the door opened. For a moment they both stood blinking, and there, equally startled, stood Mrs McPhee.

"Well, I didn't think you'd come running round bothering me!" she exclaimed. "I've been with you all the morning!"

"We're visiting Miss Murchison," said Dicky with dignity; "she's a friend of ours."

"Is she indeed! Well, she's not here; she's away on Arran in her wee summerhouse," Mrs McPhee told them crisply, and then an idea struck her. "Would she have made an appointment to photograph one of you for her advertisement firm?" she asked. "Maybe she's forgotten."

Dicky shook his head. "She didn't know we were coming *today*. Will she be away long?"

"About a month, I'd say; she's going to London next week. That's why it doesn't matter that I can only get round here for an hour every day, just polishing and keeping all the plants watered. A good thing, too, seeing as I'm needed to keep an eye on you."

They backed down the steps and prepared to go. "We'll just have to see her another day," said Dicky; "she said we could come."

Mrs McPhee was just shutting the door when Nina ran back. "Please," she said, "what are white elephants? Are they real ones, or are they just toys?"

Mrs McPhee laughed. "They're not either," she said; "they're just anything nobody has any use for. It's a name they have, but it's wonderful how many folks snaps up things that nobody wants."

"I see," said Nina, as the door closed. But she didn't.

CHAPTER SEVEN

THE BRODICK BOAT

"I really ought to mow the lawn again," murmured Mr Murray as they ate their breakfast next morning. Aunt Mary had taken a turn for the better, so things like lawns were beginning to be important again.

Dicky held his breath, and Nina gave him such a look of anguish across the table that it was a wonder Grandma didn't notice.

The children had decided that it would be much more fun if they waited till they could proudly announce that they had bought Dando for the convalescent home, before their grandparents knew anything about the jumble sale. Everything they had collected for the stall was piled in the shed, and the mower was covered in oddments, books, toys, jigsaw puzzles, and a strange assortment of hats.

But Grandma had other ideas about the lawn. "Now, don't go making yourself tired before we start," she said. "We shall be home for good in about three days, I expect, and the grass won't have turned into a field by that time."

Three days! By then, thought Nina, Dando should be theirs. He might even come and eat the grass down a little for Grandpa, before they took him as a surprise to Matron and all the children.

As soon as Mr and Mrs Murray were gone, they raced out to get the wheelbarrow. Into it they piled as much as they could, and covered it with a table-cloth. Mrs McPhee came out at that moment, shaking a duster.

"I don't know what you're playing at," she said, "but mind you put back anything you've borrowed just where it came from, and don't harm any of your grandma's things."

"We won't," promised Nina, and they made for the gate.

Mrs Wallace was as good as her word. Some undersized potatoes in small brown bags, and a perpetual calendar made of tin, already stood on the boxes in the shed. Happily, Nina scooped them up and spread the table cloth, while Dicky tipped out his load and went back for more.

By mid-morning they were ready, and a notice-board lettered in chalk leaned against the wall by the side entry. It read, "Come to our Jumbo Sale of White Elephants. All for a good cause. One penny to come in."

It seemed a long time before anyone stopped to read the notice, but Mrs Wallace paid sixpence for a worn rolling pin. The pennies rattled nicely in the tin which was to be their till, and soon, when-ever Mrs Wallace had customers, they came round to visit the sale afterwards.

By twelve o'clock they were beginning to feel that their idea was very good indeed, and their tin felt nicely heavy, when suddenly they had some un-expected customers. There was a rush of feet, and half a dozen boys jostled each other in the narrow way. Behind them, curiosity all over his freckled face, marched Jimmy Fergusson.

"Penny to come in, please," said Nina politely, and she was greeted with howls of derision.

"You've got a cheek!" shouted Jimmy, above the din. "I've been short of pocket money, but I've never tried a jumble sale!"

"It's not for us—it's for a good cause! It says so on the notice!" Dicky tried to make himself heard and to keep a dozen grubby hands off the tops and old comics at the same time.

"A penny each!" he protested. "You can't just take them—— Hi! stop them, Jimmy!"

But Jimmy was as bad as the rest. "We're a good cause!" he cried. "We need a bit of fun this morning! Who wants a hat to take home to their mum?"

Nina, her face chalky white, tried to help Dicky defend the stall, but it was useless.

"Time to scram!" yelled one of the big boys suddenly, as the bus went by and slowed for the stop. Like a flight of birds they scattered into the road. With them went comics, paperbacks, and ash-trays, as well as most of the hats, to be kicked along the pavement with whoops of glee.

Furious, Dicky tore after them, shouting, "You put those down! That's stealing!" But their legs were longer than his, and he had no breath left to shout with.

At that moment, Mrs Wallace came out to discover what the noise was.

She found Nina trembling among the wreckage, clasping the tin which held their takings. At least that was safe.

"I'll never speak to that Jimmy again! *Not* even if he says he's sorry fifty times!" she cried passionately, and when Mrs Wallace heard the name, Jimmy, she sighed.

"That one again!" she said sadly. "Always in trouble. And his folks are as nice as you could meet in a day's march. But it's my belief he's not real bad —just silly."

"He's bad!" said Nina darkly, forgetting all her prayers, as Dicky came panting back.

They looked at what was left of their treasures, and none of it seemed worth selling now.

"Better pack up—it'll be your dinner-time," Mrs Wallace told them cheerfully. "Anyway, when you count that up you'll find you have a nice postal order to send. Here's half a crown to add to it, to make up for those young ruffians coming."

She went back to the shop, and Dicky took in the notice and began sadly to pile the remaining things together. Most of them, Dicky knew, must go in Grandma's dustbin.

Neither of them spoke much as they trundled home, with the tablecloth covering the sad remnants.

"What do I hear about you playing down at Mrs Wallace's? Selling things, Mrs Knott said you were, when she spoke to me over the gate just now!" Mrs McPhee looked large and accusing as they came into the kitchen, and Dicky was too tired and dispirited to take time explaining.

"Grandma said we could go round to Mrs Wallace, if we wanted to," Nina declared truthfully, "and we weren't doing anything bad—only getting some money for a good cause, and that's not wrong; Grandma does it all the time!"

Mrs McPhee could hardly argue against that, and, as usual, her attempt at sternness was short-lived.

"Maybe, but I don't know what she'll have to say when she hears about that lark!" she said, under her breath, as she turned away to mash the potatoes.

They trailed upstairs to wash their hands, and Nina could think of nothing but Jimmy's horrible behaviour. "He's so nasty, because he never stopped to ask what it was for," she said, sniffing away her tears.

For once, Dicky didn't have a quick answer. He was remembering the time when he had done something wild and silly, and had caused the death of Nina's beloved guinea-pig. He remembered very clearly how miserable he had felt afterwards, and he wondered if Jimmy would feel the same when he stopped to think.

"I'll never forgive him. *Never!*" Nina was muttering as she squeezed the soap, and she was very surprised when Dicky said bluntly, "We'll have to; we've asked God to help him to be a

Christian—besides, we shan't be able to say, 'Forgive us our trespasses as we forgive those who trespass against us', any more, if we don't.''

Nina stared at him and stopped muttering. "I suppose we shan't," she said in a very small voice after a moment, as she thought how awful that would be.

"You don't hate me any more because your guinea-pig died," suggested Dicky, "and I know God has forgiven me for being bad that time, because I was really sorry, and we both asked Him to."

Nina watched the grubby water gurgle out of the basin, and remembered how they had both promised to follow Jesus all their lives because of His wonderful love, when He died for all the world on that first Good Friday. Hating Jimmy certainly didn't seem to fit in with that promise, and they both went down looking very thoughtful when Mrs McPhee called them to hurry.

"You two haven't been quarreling, have you?" she asked suspiciously, seeing traces of tears still on Nina's face. Nina shook her head, and Dicky said, "We don't quarrel about most things—and not today."

Neither of them wanted to tell the cause of the tears, because that would be telling tales about Jimmy, which didn't seem to fit with trying to forgive him, either.

They emptied out the money tin on Dicky's bed as soon as the meal was over. There were many more sixpences than they had realized, and the coppers sorted into dozens came to eight shillings. With their three half crowns and a little scatter of halfpennies, they had one pound five and seven-pence.

They sat and looked at each other, stirring the money round into a pool again. They both knew that one pound, five and sevenpence wouldn't buy Dando.

"Even if he was old, one of the shabby ones, I guess he'd be more than that. He might even cost five pounds," said Dicky gloomily. "We'll have to give all this money to something else, after saying it was for a good cause."

"And we've wasted lots of time when we might have been up there feeding them." Nina had a vision of the donkey field, the blue water below, and Arran in the misty distance.

"Miss Murchison!" she cried suddenly, jumping off the bed. "She's over there in a summerhouse— Mrs McPhee said so! She's jolly well known, too, with her photographs and things, so anyone would know where she was—we'd only have to ask!"

"Ask what?" Dicky looked quite blank for a moment, and then he cried, "Photographs! That's it—she pays for them! If we told her we'd raised more than one pound ourselves, she might take photos of us and pay us—she said she was always wanting children!"

Nina scooped the money back into the tin with a triumphant rattle. "It's the best idea in the world!" she cried. "But we'll have to see her quickly. She'll be in London if we wait; Mrs McPhee said that, too."

"And Grandpa and Grandma will be home soon," remembered Dicky, "so we couldn't make it a surprise. They did say we could probably get across to Arran before Mum is ready for us at the new house, so I don't see why we couldn't go by ourselves. They're too busy now to take us, and if they bring those three babies home we shan't have a chance."

Mrs McPhee was relieved that they were so quiet, and still seemed happily employed when she went off for her usual hour after lunch. They were lying on the sun-room floor, poring over a time-table. They had meant to tell her that they were going out, but she only called goodbye as she slammed the front door. The time-table gave the times of sailings from all kinds of places up and down the Clyde, but Dicky found it very hard to understand.

"The nearest place to us is Fairlie Pier," he muttered, "and that means getting the bus outside Mrs Wallace's—we'll have to go quickly because it says the boat sails at 14.15—that's a quarter past two!"

He jumped to his feet, stuffing the time-table into his pocket.

"But how will we get back? And how much does it cost?" cried Nina, alarmed at the suddenness of their departure.

"Lots of boats coming back," Dicky assured her, "and we'll be half-price, anyway. Come on—we'll miss that bus!"

"But will we be back in time for tea?" questioned Nina, as he slammed the sun-room door. He had had the presence of mind to take the money tin instead of resorting to the slow method of emptying their china pigs with the help of a knife. But the problem of teatime was one he had not foreseen, and the precious minutes were running out.

"We'll probably be back," he said, not wanting to think about the bothering idea too much. "We'll tell Mrs Wallace we're going out to tea with a friend—Miss Murchison is *sure* to give us tea."

He was already running towards the road, and Nina had a hard job to keep up. "But it's Mrs McPhee who wants to know—not Mrs Wallace."

"She'll go round to see if we're there when we don't come in, because of this morning," Dicky said with certainty, and they tore down the road as the bus lumbered into view.

Nina ran on to beg the conductor to wait a moment, while Dicky dived into the shop and gave his message to Mrs Wallace at bewildering speed. He rushed out while she was still trying to understand, and all she could do was to wave from her doorway as the bus bowled by.

"Been saving up?" asked the man in the ticket office, with amusement, when at last they reached the pier.

Dicky flushed uncomfortably. He had had to

turn the tin out on the wooden ledge, to count out enough for their fares. Over six shillings each was more than he had bargained for, and Nina looked a bit worried as she chased after sixpences which fell down and rolled away.

"Better hurry up," said the man; "she's due out now."

With a crash of copper into the tin, they set off running again. Down the sunbaked boards of the pier they raced, and were the last on board.

"Well, you nearly got left behind. A good thing you had your own tickets," said the seaman who pulled them out of the way of the gang-plank, and who obviously thought that they belonged to grown-ups already on board.

There was no need to answer; in any case, they had no breath. Now that they had done it, and the big boat was slipping out into the blue water, with gulls wheeling and crying in her wake, even Nina was excited.

They toured every deck on the vessel, and watched the islands of Big and Little Cumbrae vanish in their wake. All too soon everyone was crowding the rail as they neared their destination, to look up in delight and wonder at Goat Fell.

At last the engines were still, and they followed the other passengers down on to the pier, where cars and crates and bleating sheep waited to embark. Before them lay the green mystery of Arran.

CHAPTER EIGHT

A DOG AND A DRAINPIPE

They walked up to the end of the pier and stood looking uncertainly at the houses of Brodick close to them, and the road curving away round the bay.

Nina shivered. Higher even than the peak of Goat Fell, great clouds were massing, black and threatening. The sea was turning from blue to grey, and the gulls that cried over them sounded mournful.

Dicky glanced up at the clouds, and looked down again quickly. "There's a car with 'Taxi' on it, and the driver's just talking," he said; "I'm going to ask him where Miss Murchison is. He's sure to know."

The taxi driver stopped his conversation with an old man wheeling a barrow, and thought very hard.

"Murchison?" he said. "In Brodick? Are ye sure ye've got the right name?"

"Quite absolutely sure," Dicky told him, "and she's staying in a summerhouse, though I don't know how she can sleep there."

Suddenly, the man with the barrow looked interested. "Would ye mean Ada Murchison the portrait painter?" he asked. "She isn't in Brodick; she has a house along towards Corrie, but it's let.

Happen she's in the wee summer place at the end of her garden for a week or two, though; she canna keep away from Arran in the good weather."

"Oh, please," cried Nina, "tell us where Corrie is, because we've got to get the boat back and we'll be terribly late for tea."

"You will if you have to wait to get back to Fairlie!' said the taxi driver, with a chuckle. "You'd best jump on that bus. It's just going to pull out, but if you run you'll make it!"

Dicky heard an engine starting and they both turned and raced towards the little single-decker bus which had been filling up with people from the boat.

"Tell him you want Miss Murchison!" called the old man after them; "he'll put you off at the nearest lane."

They waved to show they understood, and scrambled up just as the bus was about to lurch away.

When Dicky told him where they wanted to be put down, the driver glanced at Nina as he punched the ticket.

"Is she going to paint that grand fair hair of yours?" he asked, which cheered them up, because other people seemed to think it was quite possible.

Soon they were driving beside cliffs on which tangled bushes grew, and on the other side of the road the sea lapped great rocks which were tumbled together as if a giant had thrown them there.

"That's the turning you want," said the driver,

as he stopped the bus suddenly. "Three houses up," he called when they had scrambled down, and they were left by the lonely roadside with only the gulls for company.

"Three houses up! Up where?" asked Nina, and then they saw that, where those rocky cliffs dipped low just beyond them, there was indeed a turning. It went upwards steeply and was very stony, but some tyre marks in a drift of muddy sand showed that cars did go up there.

They started to climb, wondering how Miss Murchison ever managed it, because she was so stout.

The banks rose high above them, and a little channel of water came all down the side of the track, making its way to some hidden culvert and out to sea.

"Guess there's a proper little burn higher up——" Dicky was saying, when a small stone came bouncing down from the heights above them and struck the road with startling force.

Another followed, and then a whole shower of shale. They both stopped and looked up. There was absolutely no one about, and nothing seemed to be stirring on the steep slope of turf and rocks which topped the bank.

And then Nina gripped Dicky's arm so tightly that he squealed. "Look!" she cried. "There's an enormous drainpipe—and feet sticking out of it!"

It took them a minute or two to find a place where they could possibly scramble up. Miss Mur-

chison was forgotten, because feet sticking out of a
drainpipe simply had to be investigated. Even the
fact that big drops of rain began splashing down
did not deter them.

It was certainly a very big pipe, and they could
clearly see the remains of another which had once
joined it, to carry water down to the channel below.
But an earth slip had smashed the lower one and
left the other like an open tunnel into the bank.

"What's he doing in there?" whispered Nina,
staring at the boy's heavy shoes and a pair of grubby
socks.

For answer, the feet began to kick vigorously, dis-
lodging more shale, but their owner showed no
signs of backing out.

At the same time a hollow shouting came from
farther up the pipe, and Dicky suddenly lurched
forward and caught the ankles and began to pull.

"He's stuck!" he cried. "He can't get out!" and
Nina pulled too.

The result was a perfect roar of shouting, but the
imprisoned boy didn't budge an inch.

"We're hurting him," said Nina, letting go. "It
would be better if we could get at him from the
other end.'"

That seemed a silly thing to say, but when they
scrambled up higher they found that the earth
and rocks had subsided farther up the pipe and
they could see the rim and a little clear space under
it.

"But it's only as big as a rabbit hole," said Dicky;

F

"we couldn't get him out of there unless he's dug out."

He lay down and squinted into the small hole. "Can you see me?" he called, and the voice, startlingly close, answered, "I'm stuck and I'll drown if it rains. Oh, do help me—quick!"

"Drown if it rains!" repeated Dicky, puzzled, as he scrambled up, and then, as the big drops turned into a sudden squall, he saw the danger.

From higher up the hill came a trickle of water down a dry gully, and it came faster and faster, sweeping round to find the lowest level, the little space in the broken pipes.

Nina saw it, too, and stood fascinated. Dicky shouted, "Quick! Make a dam—it's going to pour and we've got to turn the water down the hill!" Then she suddenly knew what she must do.

So many times they had altered the course of little streams which made their way across the beach, but now it was not a game. Tugging up lumps of turf, wrenching loose stones which hurt their hands, they tried to make a shield for the mouth of the pipe.

Dicky seized a sizeable rock and jabbed away with it, making a furrow in the earth, and seeing with relief that the water was finding it.

"Keep on! It's not enough," he panted, for, as the rain deluged down from those black clouds, the water came faster. Then an idea struck him. "I'll make a dam with myself!" he cried. "I'll lie behind our wall of turf and keep the water out—

you go and get Miss Murchison—she'll know what to do!''

"I'll go to the first house," called Nina, as she stumbled away through the rain. Slipping and sliding, she dropped into the lane, her long, wet hair almost blinding her, and her clothes covered with mud.

"Hey! Wherever have ye come from? Have ye seen my wee dog—my Angus?" said a voice, and there, coming down the way with a great grey cloak wrapped round her, was Miss Murchison.

"Oh, where can I find someone with a spade?" cried Nina, whose only thought was for Dicky, with the wet soaking into him, and for the boy who could drown in the great pipe all to easily.

"A spade? Why? You're the Murrays' child!" exclaimed Miss Murchison, but seeing the distress on Nina's face she listened, her quick mind sizing up the situation.

In a moment Nina was running again—running and scrambling in the direction which the old lady's stout stick pointed out.

Quickly she found a small croft, and three men sheltering from the rain in a dim old barn. Five minutes later help was on its way.

Miss Murchison had to remain in the lane, for the bank was far too steep for one of her size; but Nina came sliding down every few minutes to tell her how things were going, and then she scrambled up again to watch the rescue.

Three stout spades soon made a gully deep

enough to take all the water. In any case, it slackened quickly as the rainstorm swept out to sea. Then, very carefully they began to enlarge the small hole at the upper end of the pipe.

It was then that Nina came down at such a pace that she nearly fell into the lane. "It's Jimmy Fergusson!" she cried. "They told him to draw in his breath and make himself small and keep quite still, and they might draw him out feet first. But he said he couldn't, because he'd got hold of a dog, and if he let go the dog might be killed!"

"Jimmy!" cried Miss Murchison. "That Jimmy and a dog! Run, child, and ask him if it's my Angus—if that boy has pushed him down the pipe——"

Nina didn't hear the rest; she was already up to join Dicky who was helping with the widening of the hole.

Half an hour later a very muddy little procession made its way slowly up the lane, and ahead of them waddled Angus, filthy but still dignified.

"He's a grand wee dog, but he won't acknowledge his years," said the old lady. "And I'm grateful to you, young Jimmy, for getting him out of this latest pickle."

"Reckon he went in after a rat," said one of the men from the croft; "started digging, probably, and the loose rock and earth caved in on him—that's what made the wee hole show at the top end; but if this laddie hadn't gone in and held up the rock that was across his back, the poor beast would have been crushed."

Miss Murchison made clucking noises of distress, and Jimmy said cheerfully, "When they took it off and lifted Angus—then they got me out feet first quite easily."

"If you had panicked when the rain came, son, or these two had not used their heads," said one of the men, "you might never have come out at all."

"But how did you get here?" cried Nina, as she came panting up behind, finding, to her own surprise, that she was very glad indeed that Jimmy was safe. "You were with those boys this morning!" she added, but not angrily.

Jimmy looked as if he didn't want to discuss the morning very much, but Dicky answered for him.

"He ran down to Fishermen's Row and his uncle was just going away in the boat. He offered to take Jimmy over for a day of two—his Mum said he could go."

"He often does," said Jimmy, and added with a grin, "Bet he's wondering where I've got to now!"

"I have no doubt he is." Miss Murchison stopped to fetch her breath, as Angus turned in at a small garden gate. "You'd better come in and get cleaned up," she said, "and I'll get you driven home, young man. Whatever you've been up to, you heard my Angus whining, and for that heaven be praised."

They said goodbye to the crofters, who went off with their spades, past a small white house which looked like a farm, and through a garden bright with bluebells. Beyond, was a small low building, smaller than any croft they had ever seen, but it contained a bedroom, a kitchen and a studio.

"My summerhouse," explained Miss Murchison. "Most people on the island have them, and they let the proper house to summer visitors."

Nina looked round with delight. "And I thought all the time that you were in a little wooden place without a front, like Grandpa has to sit in!"

"That reminds me," said Miss Murchison, as she found soap and clean towels for her visitors. "Are Mr and Mrs Murray here on the island?—I thought they were still in Glasgow."

That question started the whole story of why they had come—the story of Dando and the grey donkeys, the Blue Bay Convalescent Home, and the jumble sale.

Miss Murchison sat down heavily on her window-seat, gathered her grubby, small dog into her lap and listened. The soap and towels lay forgotten on the table.

Suddenly Jimmy burst out, "I didn't know it was for a donkey—I only thought it was for something sissy—I didn't mean——" He stopped, his dirty face flushed with shame. "If you do buy him," he said awkwardly, "there's something I could give you for him, I reckon—just to show I'm sorry."

"Never mind that now." The old lady looked from one to the other and said abruptly, "Do you know what donkeys cost?"

It was Dicky's turn to flush. "We guessed," he said slowly. "We guessed five pounds, and we came over to ask you if you could photograph us like you do the other children, and then we could make it up."

The grey eyes twinkled. "You have a good business brain," said Miss Murchison. "It's fortunate that I have a telephone."

While they washed, she left them and went across to the big house, and she was gone some time. The children fell silent after she had left; now that the excitement of the rescue was over, the memory of the morning's events made them all feel uncomfortable.

Suddenly Jimmy burst out, "I know you hate me, but I'll never do anything like that again—not *ever*! It was funny at the time, with all the boys laughing, but while I was coming over here in Uncle's boat I kept thinking about it. I knew it was mean—and—and God must be angry with me."

"But you don't believe in God—or Jesus!" cried Dicky, and Jimmy sat, kicking his toes against the chair leg and staring at the ground.

"I said I didn't because I didn't want to," he said slowly, "but inside I knew it was true, all the time. When I went looking for herons this afternoon I climbed up above the lane and sat on the rocks there, and I felt horribly lonely. So after a bit I asked God to forgive me—and—and to help me to tell you I was sorry—and then I heard Angus yelping and I got into the pipe to find him."

"So you're going to follow Jesus now and

always?" cried Nina, her eyes very bright.

Jimmy looked up with a broad grin on his freckled face, "I know I belong now!" he told them. "When I was in that beastly pipe I wondered if I was stuck there for good when I found I couldn't wriggle out. The earth began to shift, and poor old Angus was nearly getting squashed, so I couldn't let go of the bit of rock I was holding off him. Then I remembered a hymn that my mum sings sometimes—it's something about, 'Oh, love that will not let me go'. I reckoned Jesus wouldn't let me go, either, if I asked to belong to Him—and then I wasn't really afraid any more."

"So God did find a way, like Miss Murchison said," whispered Nina, but only Dicky heard her.

When their old friend returned, she had an armfull of clean jeans and jerseys. "A good thing my visitors have children," she said as she dumped them on the table. "Get changed; we're going for a drive."

The sky was blue again as they ran out into the garden, and the hills and fields all round glowed with bright colour and freshness after rain.

"Get in," said Miss Murchison, and they were all a bit astonished to see her at the wheel of an ancient car, with Angus seated on a mackintosh beside her. As she drove, she told them several things —first, that she had rung up the convalescent home and made certain that Miss Henderson would really welcome a donkey; next, that she had spoken to Mr Ross, who was willing to part with Dando, but only to a good home. "And for twenty pounds," added Miss Murchison, as she took the car up an impossibly steep hill with the greatest of ease.

"Twenty pounds!" gasped all three children, and Nina's heart sank. "Oh, dear!" she said. "I don't think we'll ever——"

"Yes, you will," said the old lady briskly. "We will make a business arrangement. When your hair has the mud washed out of it, young lady, I think you could be very useful. And you boys—you have a certain horrible attraction."

She chuckled as Jimmy cried in panic, "Not me—I couldn't sit still and look pretty!"

Nina was in a daze of happiness. The car climbed higher and higher, and on every side the mountains rose, blue and purple and magnificent. Great sheets of gorse and broom blazed at the roadside, and almost every turn showed glimpses of the sea.

"And here's your uncle's croft," said Miss Murchison to Jimmy; "we mustn't be here long, for I've arranged that these two shall go back on a friend's cabin cruiser. It's anchored down there by the pier, and he'll be ready in half an hour."

"But is the last steamer gone?" cried Dicky. "There was one later."

"Did you look at your time-table properly?" asked Miss Murchison. "I think not. If you had looked at what all the little letters mean, you would have seen there wasn't one at all after yours went back."

"So that's what the taxi man meant!" said Nina under her breath.

"And where do you think you've been?" roared a voice as Jimmy tumbled from the car. A tall, bony man appeared from beside a stone wall where he had been sawing logs, but Miss Murchison leaned out and began defending Jimmy with vigour. "You've got a brave laddie for a nephew," she said, as she finished the story of Angus in the pipe. "Well, I must get these children back to their grandparents!" she added as she began turning the car, leaving the man quite speechless.

At that moment, the sound of flying feet made them look towards the croft behind him. Jimmy came running down the path and was waving them to wait. "It's a little saddle!" he cried, "—a baby's one—and I had it when I used to ride old moke up here years ago. It's mine to give, isn't it, Uncle? You said I could have it once, and it only hangs up in the byre."

"Well, I'm fair staggered!" was all his uncle said, as Jimmy pushed his gift through the car window to Dicky.

"The very thing for the lightweights that Dando will carry in the beginning," said Miss Murchison, looking very pleased.

The tiny saddle was made of thick felt, and had just a webbing girth, and no stirrups. Obviously it was meant for a baby who would be held on.

Nina clasped it to her in a happy dream. Jimmy should come with them to fetch the donkey from

Mr Ross's farm, she decided.

"He's got a lot of niceness inside him, and now he belongs to Jesus he'll let it get out," she thought.

Dicky's voice brought her back to the present. "Herons!" he was saying. "Jimmy said he was looking for herons this afternoon!"

"And he had a good chance of seeing some; I know just where they feed," answered their old friend. She glanced at her watch, and as they turned on to the coast road she drove more slowly.

"There!" she said suddenly, coming almost to a stop.

"Where? I can't see," Nina craned over Dicky's shoulder as he gazed spellbound at the brown rocks by the edge of the sea. And then something moved slightly, and she gave a little gasp of joy. Slender and grey, a tall heron was fishing in a pool, and while they watched it rose, and flapped silently away.

"Grandpa would have loved that," said Dicky thoughtfully, as the car started up again. Then a wave of anxiety swamped Nina. What was Grandma going to say when they got home?

"It's just on seven," said Miss Murchison, as though she read her thoughts. "You won't be over late for the folks from Glasgow, and I've spoken to Mrs McPhee already. You owe her an apology, mind, for not coming in to your tea, and causing her worry. I think maybe she'll forgive you, though, when she hears all about it. Take her to see Dando one day, with that little saddle on him!"

The blue and white motor-boat was rocking gently by the jetty, and Miss Murchison went ahead of them to greet her friend.

"Two passengers for the mainland!" she said cheerfully. "I'd think it a kindness if you went home with them when you get ashore, and take them safely to Mr and Mrs Murray."

"Aye aye, Ma'am!" laughed the bearded man, as he reached up to steady Nina.

"It's been wizard—every minute of it!" said Dicky, with a huge sigh of satisfaction as they headed out to sea. And then he added cheerfully, "Now that Dando's settled we'll have time to take Jimmy up the glen, and have a proper look at that old dipper."